Kelly's Secret

Elizabeth opened her eyes and sat up in her bed. It was the middle of the night, and a noise had woken her up. It sounded like someone was crying.

Elizabeth switched on the lamp on her night table. Kelly was curled up in the guest bed. She was crying. Elizabeth got out of bed and sat down on the edge of the cot.

"What's wrong?" Elizabeth asked.

Jessica woke up and came over, too. "Why are you crying, Kelly?"

Instead of answering, their cousin just started crying harder.

Jessica and Elizabeth looked at each other. They both knew they were thinking the same thing.

What was wrong with

Bantam Skylark Books in the
  SWEET VALLEY KIDS series
Ask your bookseller for the
  books you have missed

SWEET VALLEY KIDS

COUSIN KELLY'S FAMILY SECRET

Written by
Molly Mia Stewart

Created by
FRANCINE PASCAL

Illustrated by
Ying-Hwa Hu

A BANTAM SKYLARK BOOK®
NEW YORK · TORONTO · LONDON · SYDNEY · AUCKLAND

To Rachel Amanda Arlook

RL 2, 005–008

COUSIN KELLY'S FAMILY SECRET
A Bantam Skylark Book / November 1991

*Sweet Valley High® and Sweet Valley Kids are trademarks of
Francine Pascal*

Conceived by Francine Pascal

*Produced by Daniel Weiss Associates, Inc.
33 West 17th Street
New York, NY 10011*

Cover art by Susan Tang

ISBN 0-553-15920-8

Published simultaneously in the United States and Canada

*Bantam Books are published by Bantam Books, a division of Bantam
Doubleday Dell Publishing Group, Inc. Its trademark, consisting of the
words "Bantam Books" and the portrayal of a rooster, is Registered in U.S.
Patent and Trademark Office and in other countries. Marca Registrada.
Bantam Books, 666 Fifth Avenue, New York, New York 10103.*

PRINTED IN THE UNITED STATES OF AMERICA

CWO   0 9 8 7 6 5 4 3 2 1

CHAPTER 1

Kelly's Coming!

"My turkey is going to have red and blue feathers," Elizabeth Wakefield said, drawing an outline of her hand on a piece of construction paper.

Her twin sister, Jessica, looked up from across the art table. "Turkeys don't have blue feathers," she said.

"Mine does." Elizabeth drew legs on her turkey. "My turkey can be any color I want it to be."

Elizabeth had a vivid imagination. She loved reading books and daydreaming about magic carpet rides and talking animals.

Sometimes she pretended to be a super-star athlete when she played soccer. She loved school, and she always got good grades because she worked hard in her classes.

Jessica was different from her sister in many ways. Instead of reading, she enjoyed playing dress-up and going to modern dance class. She didn't like playing outside very much, because her clothes got too dirty. Jessica thought that the best thing about school was passing notes and talking to her friends.

Jessica and Elizabeth had a lot of things in common, though. For one thing, they looked exactly alike. Both girls had blue-green eyes and long blond hair with bangs. They shared a bedroom, and toys, and chores. Sometimes they could even read each other's thoughts and finish each other's sentences.

Elizabeth and Jessica were best friends, and they both thought that being twins was the best thing in the world.

"I hope we don't have a blue turkey for Thanksgiving dinner," Jessica said. "Yuck."

"Hey, Jessica," Lila Fowler said. She was Jessica's best friend after Elizabeth. "Isn't your cousin coming for Thanksgiving?"

Jessica nodded. "Her name is Kelly Bates. She's coming tonight."

"I can't wait," Elizabeth said.

"It's only Monday. What's Kelly going to do tomorrow and Wednesday while you're at school?" asked Eva Simpson.

"She's going to come to school with us," Jessica explained. "Wait until you see her. She looks so much like us, she could almost be another twin."

"Thanksgiving isn't until Thursday. How

come she's coming so early?" Amy Sutton asked, messily coloring in her turkey's tail. "Does she live far away?"

Elizabeth picked out a sky-blue crayon. "She lives about two hours away. Aunt Laura is bringing Kelly tonight before dinner, and then she and Uncle Greg are coming on Thanksgiving Day."

"But why is Kelly coming early?" Lila asked.

"Just because," Jessica answered with a shrug.

Elizabeth frowned. She wasn't sure why Kelly was coming early. It meant Aunt Laura had to make an extra trip to bring her. Elizabeth hadn't really thought about it much, because she was so glad she and Jessica would have extra time to play with Kelly.

4

"There has to be a reason," Lila said in her know-it-all voice. "Nobody does things for no reason."

"Jessica does," Ellen Riteman said, pointing at Jessica. "Look, she just colored her fingernails with purple crayon for no reason."

Jessica made a face at Ellen. "I had a reason. I did it because my nails look pretty that way," she said. She held up her hands for everyone to see.

"Anyway, what difference does it make if Kelly is coming early?" Eva asked, smiling. "It'll be fun to meet her."

Elizabeth smiled, too. She hadn't seen Kelly in more than a year, and she couldn't wait for the visit to start.

When Elizabeth and Jessica got home from school, they ran straight upstairs to their bedroom. "This place is a mess!" Jessica said.

"Only your half of the room," Elizabeth pointed out. "As usual."

"You'll help me clean up, won't you?" Jessica asked. "Pretty please?"

Elizabeth picked up a toy koala bear from the floor and tossed it onto her sister's bed. "Of course I will, but only so Kelly doesn't have to stay in a pig sty!"

"Oink! Oink!" Jessica said, tossing a stuffed animal at Elizabeth and laughing. Then the twins got to work and straightened up. Kelly would be sharing their room with them, so they really did want it to be neat and clean.

"Let's get the extra bed out," Elizabeth said when they were finished.

A folding cot on wheels was stored in the

hall closet. The girls pushed it into their room and opened it up.

"Maybe Mom and Dad will let us stay up late," Jessica said, flopping onto the guest bed.

"Or we can play guessing games in the dark," Elizabeth suggested.

"Elizabeth! Jessica!" Mrs. Wakefield called from downstairs. "Kelly's here!"

CHAPTER 2

No Appetite

Jessica and Elizabeth raced down the stairs just as their mother opened the front door. "Hi!" they both yelled as Aunt Laura walked in.

"Hi, girls," Aunt Laura said, putting down the suitcase she was carrying.

"Where's Kelly?" Jessica asked.

Kelly stepped out from behind her mother. She smiled shyly at the twins. "Hi," she said.

"Hi, Laura. Hi, Kelly," Mrs. Wakefield said, giving them each a kiss. Aunt Laura was Mrs. Wakefield's sister.

"Why don't you take your things upstairs,"

Aunt Laura suggested to Kelly. "I'll bet Elizabeth and Jessica have a lot of new toys to show you."

Kelly nodded. "OK," she said quietly.

"Come on," Elizabeth said. She took Kelly's hand, and Jessica picked up her suitcase. "Let's go."

"I can't wait to show you my new doll," Jessica said as they went upstairs. "She's got red hair that grows when I push her belly button."

"And I have some new books," Elizabeth added. "Have you read *Sailor Seagull*?"

Kelly entered the twins' bedroom and sat on the guest bed. "No, I haven't," she said.

Jessica was surprised that Kelly didn't seem happy to see them. She decided to be extra-friendly. "Did you bring any toys?" she asked. "If you didn't, you can play with ours."

10

"Thanks," Kelly said, smiling.

"We're really glad you're here," Elizabeth told her.

"Why did you come early?" Jessica asked. Lila's questions in school had made her curious.

Instantly, Kelly's smile disappeared. "No special reason," she whispered, looking down.

Elizabeth's eyes widened. "Is something wrong?"

"No," Kelly said quickly.

Jessica thought that Kelly seemed sad, even though she said nothing was wrong. Maybe she was just a little bit homesick.

"Let's play triplets," Jessica suggested. "I told everyone in our class that you look just like us. Maybe we could fool people into thinking we're triplets." She ran to the mir-

12

ror. "Come over here," she said to Elizabeth and Kelly.

When the three girls stood in front of the mirror, they did almost look like triplets. Kelly also had blond hair and blue eyes, and her face looked a lot like Jessica's and Elizabeth's. They all smiled, and that made them look even more alike.

"We could make up a play," Elizabeth suggested. "We could be the three little pigs."

"Or the three billy goats gruff," Kelly said.

"Or the three musketeers!" Jessica shouted.

They began a pretend sword fight. Jessica jumped onto her bed. "Take that and that!" she said, stabbing the air with her imaginary sword.

"You got me!" Kelly groaned.

"Ahh!" Elizabeth yelled. She grabbed her stomach and fell to the floor.

Jessica fell on her bed and pretended to die. "The end," she said.

"Kelly! I'm leaving now!" Aunt Laura called.

Kelly stood up and ran out of the room. She had a worried expression on her face.

"Does Kelly seem sad to you?" Elizabeth asked her sister.

"I don't know. If something's wrong, maybe she'll tell us about it later," Jessica said. "Let's see if dinner's ready yet. I'm starving."

At dinner, Kelly sat next to Steven, the twins' older brother. "Mom made all your special favorites," he said. "Luckily for me, they're my favorites, too."

Jessica glanced at Kelly's plate. Fried

14

chicken, rice, and peas *were* all Kelly's favorite foods, but Kelly wasn't eating very much.

"Aren't you hungry, Kelly?" Mr. Wakefield asked. "How about some more rice?"

"No, thank you," Kelly said politely.

"Would you like another glass of milk?" Mrs. Wakefield asked.

Kelly shook her head. "No, thanks."

Jessica noticed Mr. and Mrs. Wakefield sharing a worried look. She put a forkful of peas in her mouth and chewed slowly.

What was wrong with Kelly? she wondered.

CHAPTER 3

A Sleepless Night

Elizabeth opened her eyes and sat up in bed. It was the middle of the night, and a noise had woken her up. She listened for a minute. It sounded like someone was crying.

"Kelly? Is that you?" she whispered.

Kelly didn't answer, but the crying sounds continued.

"What is it?" Jessica asked in a sleepy voice.

Elizabeth switched on the lamp on her night table. Kelly was curled up in the guest bed. She was crying. Elizabeth got out of bed and sat down on the edge of the cot.

"What's wrong, Kelly?" Elizabeth asked. "You can tell us, whatever it is."

Jessica came over, too. "Why are you crying?"

Instead of answering, their cousin just started crying harder.

"Kelly, don't cry. It's OK," Elizabeth said anxiously. "Did you have a bad dream?"

"I'm getting Mom," Jessica said. She hurried out of the room.

Elizabeth tried to comfort Kelly, but no matter what she said, Kelly wouldn't stop crying. Elizabeth began to feel like crying herself.

"What is it?" Mrs. Wakefield asked, coming into the room in her nightgown and robe. She sat on the cot, took Kelly into her arms, and started rocking her. "There, there," she whispered.

18

Elizabeth and Jessica stood and stared. It was terrible to see their cousin sobbing so hard.

"What's wrong with her, Mom?" Jessica asked.

Steven appeared in the doorway, rubbing his eyes. "What's going on?" he asked sleepily. "Is Kelly sick?"

"I guess I should tell you," Mrs. Wakefield said quietly. She had a very serious look on her face. "Aunt Laura and Uncle Greg are not happy being married to each other anymore."

Elizabeth gulped. "Oh, no!" she whispered.

"Why not?" Jessica asked, wide-eyed.

Mrs. Wakefield looked sad. "They're not sure they love each other anymore, and they might decide to get a divorce. That means they wouldn't be married to each other anymore."

Kelly sobbed even louder. Mrs. Wakefield smoothed Kelly's hair. "There, there, sweetheart."

"Are Aunt Laura and Uncle Greg really going to get a divorce?" Elizabeth asked.

"They're not sure yet," Mrs. Wakefield said. "They wanted to have a couple of days to themselves to talk it over. That's why Kelly came early, and it's also why you kids need to be especially nice to her while she's here. I want you to give her the royal treatment."

"We will," Elizabeth said quickly. Jessica and Steven nodded.

"One more thing," Mrs. Wakefield said. "This is a private, family problem. I don't want you to discuss it with your friends. It would upset Kelly even more if everyone started asking her questions."

"We promise," the twins said at the same time.

Kelly had almost stopped crying by now. "How do you feel, honey?" Mrs. Wakefield asked her.

"Better," Kelly said with a sniffle.

"Do you think you'll be able to go to sleep now?" Mrs. Wakefield asked.

Kelly sniffed again and nodded. "I'll try."

Elizabeth looked at Jessica while their mother tucked Kelly in. "I feel so bad for her," Elizabeth whispered. "I wish there was something we could do to make her feel better, don't you?"

"Yes," Jessica whispered back. "But what can we do?"

Elizabeth shook her head. She didn't know. Kelly's problem was an awfully big one.

CHAPTER 4

Three Peas in a Pod

"Wake up, sleepyheads!" Mrs. Wakefield said cheerfully.

Jessica opened her eyes. Her mother was pulling up the window shades. "Hi, Mom," Jessica said with a yawn.

"Did Kelly wake up again last night?" Mrs. Wakefield asked Jessica in a whisper.

"I don't think so," Jessica whispered back. She looked over at her cousin and called out, "Time to get up!"

Kelly sat up and stretched. "Good morning," she said.

Elizabeth opened her eyes, pushed her

covers back, and jumped out of bed. "Good morning, everyone!" she said.

"Hurry up and get ready for school, girls," Mrs. Wakefield said as she left the room. "Breakfast is in exactly six minutes and fourteen seconds."

Kelly laughed. Jessica was glad to see that her cousin seemed happier this morning.

"I have a great idea," Jessica said, getting out of bed. "Let's all wear matching clothes. That way we'll really look like triplets."

Elizabeth opened their closet. "But we don't all have the same outfits, do we?"

"I brought jeans," Kelly said. "And some T-shirts."

"Great," Jessica said. "I love wearing jeans and T-shirts." That wasn't exactly true. Jessica usually preferred to wear pretty

24

skirts and dresses to school. But she wanted to give Kelly the royal treatment.

When they were all dressed in jeans and blue T-shirts, they ran down the stairs to the kitchen.

"I can't believe my eyes," Mr. Wakefield said, looking up from his newspaper. "Three peas in a pod."

"No, we're the three musketeers," Kelly said, laughing. She sat down at the kitchen table and poured herself some cereal.

Jessica and Elizabeth looked at each other. The twins knew they would have to make sure their cousin stayed this happy all day.

After breakfast, the girls got their school-books and headed for the bus stop. "Wait until everyone sees us," Jessica said.

Caroline Pearce spotted them first. "Wow! Look at you!" she said with a gasp.

The kids at the bus stop crowded around Jessica, Elizabeth, and Kelly. "I can't believe how much you look like them, Kelly," said Crystal Burton, a third grader.

"I told you she did," Jessica said proudly. She loved being the center of attention.

"Kelly doesn't look *exactly* like Elizabeth and Jessica," Todd Wilkins said, studying their faces carefully. "But you sure could fool a lot of people."

Kelly didn't say much, but Jessica could tell her cousin liked all the attention as much as she did. When the bus came, Jessica and Elizabeth argued over who would get to sit with Kelly. Kelly finally chose by playing eenie-meenie-miney-mo, and Jessica won.

At school, the twins introduced Kelly to their teacher, Mrs. Otis. Mrs. Otis already knew that Kelly would be attending her class for two days.

"Welcome to Sweet Valley Elementary," Mrs. Otis said with a smile. "Let's see if we can find an empty desk for you."

"I hope you can sit near me," Jessica whispered to her cousin. It made her feel good to know she was helping to cheer up Kelly.

Elizabeth and Kelly followed Mrs. Otis, but Jessica stayed near the door. She could see Lila coming down the hall.

"Is she here?" Lila asked as soon as she saw Jessica.

"Yes," Jessica replied. "And we're giving her the royal treatment. It's fun."

"Royal treatment?" Lila said. "Why?"

"Just—just because she's a guest," Jessica said, remembering her promise of secrecy.

Lila looked curious. "Did you find out why she had to come early?"

"No." Jessica said quickly.

"Really?" Lila said. "That's funny."

Jessica didn't answer. But from the look on Lila's face, Jessica was sure Lila knew she had a secret.

CHAPTER 5

Jessica's Big Mouth

"Pssst," Todd whispered to Elizabeth. Elizabeth turned around. It was almost time for recess. "What is it?"

"My family's going on a ski trip during winter vacation," he said.

"Skiing?" Jessica asked, overhearing him. She grinned. "You'll probably fall down and turn into a big snowball."

"You're the one who'll be a snowball," Todd told Jessica.

Elizabeth stared at him. "What do you mean?"

"Nothing," Todd said mysteriously. "But I know something that you don't."

The recess bell rang. Elizabeth was eager to find out what Todd was talking about, but right now her cousin was more important. "Come on, Kelly. Come on, Jessica," she said. "Let's go."

"I'll follow you in a minute," Jessica told her. "Lila asked me to wait for her."

Elizabeth led the way to the playground. "Do you want to go on the seesaw?" she asked her cousin.

"Sure." Kelly had a thoughtful look on her face, but she smiled at Elizabeth.

"Or we could play jump rope," Elizabeth said. "Or climb on the jungle gym." She wanted to make sure they did Kelly's favorite thing. Elizabeth hoped that that would help to keep Kelly's mind off her worries.

32

"Sure, any of those things would be fun," Kelly said. She pointed to the swings. "Then later, maybe we could go on the swings."

"Let's do that first," Elizabeth replied instantly. She took Kelly's hand. Together, they ran to the swings and found two next to each other.

"Mrs. Otis is a nice teacher," Kelly said. "You're lucky."

"I know," Elizabeth said. She pushed off so that the two of them were swinging back and forth at the same time. She could tell Kelly was having fun.

Kelly looked across the playground. "Is the girl talking to Jessica named Lila?" she asked.

"Yes," Elizabeth said with a grin. "I call her Miss Know-It-All."

Lila and Jessica were walking toward the

33

swing set. Amy, Eva, and Ellen were with them.

"We were just talking about you," Lila said to Kelly, giving her a friendly smile.

Elizabeth and Kelly let their swings slow down. "What about?" Elizabeth asked.

"I'm curious about something," Lila said.

"How come you had to come early for Thanksgiving?" Lila wanted to know.

Elizabeth looked quickly at her cousin. Lila was spoiling the day.

"Do you have to know everything?" Jessica spoke up suddenly. "Her parents might be getting divorced, and they had to be alone to talk about it, so leave her alone, OK?"

"Jessica!" Elizabeth shouted.

Everyone was silent for a few seconds. Jessica bit her lip. "I didn't mean to say any-

34

thing, Kelly," she said. "I'm—I'm really sorry."

"Are your parents really getting divorced?" Ellen asked.

"Crystal Burton's parents got divorced," Lila said in a hushed voice. "They used to fight all the time."

Eva looked sad. "That's really terrible news, Kelly."

"Who are you going to live with?" Amy asked.

"It's none of your business," Jessica said.

Elizabeth was so angry with Jessica that she wanted to scream. She could see that Kelly was getting more upset by the second. "There's a good show on television tonight," she said. "It's about elephants."

"Crystal Burton only sees her father every

other weekend," Ellen said. "And for three weeks in the summer."

"Did anyone read that chapter in our science book?" Elizabeth asked loudly. She wished they would all stop talking about divorce!

"I really feel sorry for you, Kelly," Amy said.

So far, Kelly had not said a word. But her eyes were filled with tears. Finally, she began to cry. She jumped off her swing and ran away.

"I didn't mean to tell." Jessica sniffed.

Elizabeth scowled at Jessica. Then she ran after Kelly.

CHAPTER 6

Lila's Idea

Jessica sat down on one of the swings. "I'm so dumb," she said in a gloomy voice. "Why couldn't I keep my big mouth shut?"

"Was it supposed to be a secret?" Lila asked.

"Yes." Jessica dragged her feet along the ground. "Now Kelly's crying, and it's all my fault. What should I do?"

Lila sat down next to her. "I don't know."

"You should just say you're sorry," Ellen suggested.

"She already did that," Lila said.

"I have to do something to make it up to her," Jessica said.

Lila jumped to her feet. "I've got an idea," she said excitedly. "Crystal Burton's parents got divorced, right?"

"So? I don't want to have to cheer her up, too," Jessica complained.

"No, you don't have to, because she's not unhappy," Lila said. "She told me she's glad they did."

The other girls stared at her in surprise. "Glad?" Eva asked.

"I'll go get her." Lila ran toward the other side of the playground.

"I don't know what makes that such a good idea," Jessica grumbled. She glanced over her shoulder. Elizabeth and Kelly were slowly walking back toward the swing set. Kelly wasn't crying anymore, but she still looked sad.

The others were quiet. When Elizabeth

and Kelly reached them, Jessica gave Kelly a hug. "I'm sorry," she whispered.

"That's OK," Kelly said softly.

"Here come Lila and Crystal," Ellen said.

Jessica crossed her fingers behind her back. She hoped Lila's idea worked.

"Hi, Kelly," Lila began. She nudged Crystal. "Crystal wants to tell you something."

Kelly looked surprised.

"My parents got divorced last year," Crystal explained. "I was upset when they first told me, but now we're all a lot happier."

"Really?" Kelly sounded uncertain.

Crystal nodded quickly. "They used to fight all the time, and that really scared me. But now that they don't live together, they get along much better."

"Who do you live with?" Kelly asked.

"My mother," Crystal answered. "But I see

41

my dad on weekends. And I can call him whenever I want."

"Wow," Jessica said. "That's great. See, Kelly, it wouldn't be so bad even if your parents got divorced."

Kelly shook her head. "But I don't want them to. Even if it made them stop fighting."

"I know how you feel," Crystal said. "But it turned out OK for me."

Jessica watched her cousin's expression hopefully. But Lila's idea didn't seem to have worked very well.

More than anything, Jessica wished she had not blurted out Kelly's secret. It was just that secrets were so hard to keep.

"I just thought of something," Jessica said, lowering her voice.

Kelly and Elizabeth looked curious. "What?" Elizabeth asked.

"Remember how Todd was acting really mysterious about his family's ski vacation?" Jessica said. "Kelly, can you try to find out what he's hiding?"

"From Todd?" Kelly started to smile. "I could pretend to be a detective."

"That's right!" Jessica said happily. "But don't let him know you're going to tell us."

Kelly gave Jessica a big smile. "Oh, I won't," she promised. "I'll go ask him now. I see him over there by the jungle gym."

After Kelly had walked away, Jessica let out a sigh of relief. "Whew. It's a hard job trying to cheer up someone all the time."

"But it's worth it," Elizabeth said. "I just hope we can really do it.

Jessica crossed her fingers again. "Me, too."

CHAPTER 7

Kelly's New Secret

"What a delicious dinner," Mr. Wakefield said that night after they had finished eating. "What's for dessert?"

"Ice cream," Mrs. Wakefield said.

"My favorite!" Jessica shouted.

"Mine, too," Kelly said.

"I'll get it," Elizabeth offered.

"Kelly and your father and I will have our ice cream in the TV room," Mrs. Wakefield announced. "You three can clear the table and put the dishes in the dishwasher."

"Rats," Jessica said.

Elizabeth kicked her under the table. "OK," she said, giving Kelly a friendly smile.

While Mr. and Mrs. Wakefield and Kelly took their ice cream into the den, Elizabeth, Jessica, and Steven cleared the table. Elizabeth thought it was nice of her mother to give Kelly such extra-special treatment.

"I can't believe we have to do chores before we even get our dessert," Jessica grumbled. "That stinks."

"Kelly's getting the royal treatment, because Aunt Laura and Uncle Greg might be getting divorced," Elizabeth reminded her, putting the plates in the sink. "Do you want to trade places?"

"No way!" Jessica said. She made a face. "I'd rather do chores all day than be in Kelly's place."

"Me, too," Elizabeth said. "I think it would

be awful if Mom and Dad ever stopped loving each other."

"There's a kid in my class whose parents are getting divorced," Steven said as he put the butter dish in the refrigerator. "I was at his house once, and they weren't speaking to each other. It was horrible."

"You'd better not mention that in front of Kelly," Elizabeth said, looking quickly at the door. "She gets upset when people talk about divorce."

"I'm not that dumb," Steven said. "I know better than to talk about it in front of her."

Jessica looked at the floor. She still felt terrible about blurting out Kelly's secret that day at school.

"Listen," Elizabeth said. "We have to think of a really good plan for cheering up Kelly."

"Right," Jessica agreed. "Something that

will make her so happy she'll forget all about her parents."

Steven made a face. "Well, at least for a little while."

"I don't know what—" Jessica began.

"Shh, here she comes," Elizabeth whispered.

Kelly walked into the kitchen with her empty ice cream bowl. "I'll help you with the dishes," she said.

"No, you don't have to," Steven said.

"We're almost finished," Elizabeth added. "Hey, you never told us what Todd said."

"Todd?" Kelly put her dish in the sink. "What do you mean?"

"You know," Jessica said. "What's his secret?"

Kelly smiled mysteriously. "You mean, *our* secret."

"What?" Elizabeth's mouth dropped open. "You found out, and you won't tell?"

"We'll tickle you until you do," Jessica warned. She took a step closer to Kelly.

"No!" Kelly giggled and dodged away.

Elizabeth, Jessica, and Steven began chasing Kelly around the kitchen. Kelly screamed and laughed as she tried to get away. At last, Steven caught her and held her by both arms.

"I'll never tell," Kelly said, breathing hard.

Elizabeth wanted to know the secret, but she could see that Kelly was having fun keeping it from them.

Jessica held up one finger. "Do you see this? This is my tickling finger."

"No!" Kelly shrieked, giggling wildly.

Just then, the telephone rang. Mrs. Wakefield answered it in the den.

"Kelly!" she called. "It's your mom and dad."

Kelly's smile disappeared instantly. Steven let go of her arms. Kelly looked so scared and worried that Elizabeth felt her stomach do a flip-flop.

"I'm coming," Kelly said, walking to the door.

She left the kitchen. Elizabeth, Jessica, and Steven looked at each other. They knew there was nothing they could do.

CHAPTER 8

We Love You

"Did they decide?" Jessica asked as Mr. and Mrs. Wakefield came into the kitchen.

"They just called to say hello," Mrs. Wakefield said. "They had planned to call tonight."

"So there's no bad news?" Elizabeth wanted to know.

Mr. Wakefield smiled. "Well, people say no news is good news."

Jessica sat in her chair at the kitchen table. She looked worried.

"Mom? Dad?" she began nervously. "You wouldn't ever get a divorce, would you?"

"Oh, honey," Mrs. Wakefield said. She and Mr. Wakefield sat down at the table, too. "Of course not. Why would you even wonder about that?"

Jessica took a deep breath. It was a difficult subject to talk about. "Sometimes you and Dad get into arguments."

"Just because we have disagreements, doesn't mean Mom and I don't love each other," Mr. Wakefield said, looking around at the twins and Steven.

"That's right, kids." Mrs. Wakefield took Jessica's hand and squeezed it. "Married people can disagree about things. All it means is that they have different opinions, and that's normal."

"Like the way Jessica and I don't always want to play the same game after school?" Elizabeth asked.

Their mother nodded. "That's right. It doesn't mean you don't love each other."

Jessica looked at Elizabeth and nodded. "That's true."

"And when you disagree with us," Steven added, "it doesn't mean you don't love us."

"That's right, Steven," Mr. Wakefield said. "It's normal to disagree. People are all different, so they have different ideas about things."

"When you love someone, you try to make decisions that will satisfy both of you," Mrs. Wakefield explained. She smiled at Mr. Wakefield.

"Why is it different with Aunt Laura and Uncle Greg?" Elizabeth asked.

Mrs. Wakefield shook her head slowly. "They just disagree on too many things. And the things they argue about are much more serious than where to go for vacation or what kind of car to buy. They aren't sure they can settle their disagreements anymore."

Jessica put her chin in her hands. There was a lot to think about. But it was a relief for her to hear her parents explain it all, and to know that they loved each other.

"So remember," Mr. Wakefield said. "Kelly is very upset and worried. Let her know how much you love her. That's all we can do for her right now."

"Mom?" Jessica spoke up. "Can we sleep in the fold-out sofa bed in the den tonight?"

Mrs. Wakefield looked puzzled. "Why?"

"Because it's such a big bed that Liz and Kelly and I could all sleep in it together," Jessica said.

Elizabeth clapped her hands. "That's a great idea!"

"Of course," Mrs. Wakefield agreed, smiling at Jessica. "It is a great idea."

"Come on, Liz," Jessica suggested. "Let's go see if she's off the phone yet."

The twins walked into the den. Kelly was just hanging up the telephone.

"Hi," Elizabeth said softly.

Kelly looked at them. "They said they didn't decide anything yet."

"We're keeping our fingers crossed," Jessica promised. She crossed her fingers on both hands and held them up.

Elizabeth began taking the cushions off the big couch. "Let's open this up. Mom said all three of us could sleep here tonight."

"Why?" Kelly asked. She seemed very upset and tired. She yawned sleepily and rubbed her eyes.

Jessica walked over to Kelly and hugged

her. "Because we want to sleep three in a bed, just like three peas in a pod."

"OK," Kelly said, trying to smile.

The girls went upstairs to change into their pajamas and get their pillows. Then Elizabeth and Jessica opened up the bed, and Mrs. Wakefield brought in sheets and blankets.

"We can talk in bed until it's time to go to sleep," Elizabeth said, climbing in. "Kelly gets to be in the middle."

When all three girls were settled in the big bed together, Jessica took Kelly's hand. "We love you," she said.

"You do?" Kelly looked from Jessica to Elizabeth and back again.

"We really do," Elizabeth said, squeezing Kelly's other hand.

Kelly smiled and let out a tired sigh. Then her eyes closed, and she fell asleep.

CHAPTER 9

Elizabeth's Plan

After school on Wednesday, Elizabeth, Kelly, and Jessica went to the park. Thinking about the words "royal treatment" had given Elizabeth an idea.

"I have to go talk to some of the other kids," she told Jessica and Kelly. "I'll be back in a couple of minutes."

She ran over to the jungle gym. Amy, Eva, Todd, Ken Matthews, and Winston Egbert were all there. "I have to ask a favor," she told them. "Jessica and I need you all to help us cheer up Kelly."

"Sure," Amy said as she hung upside

down. Her ponytail almost brushed the ground. "What is it?"

"I don't want to sing a song or anything," Ken warned.

"No, it's nothing like that," Elizabeth said. "I want to make Kelly the Queen of the Park."

Eva laughed. "It's a good thing Lila isn't here. She thinks she's the queen."

"That sounds like fun," Winston told Elizabeth. He made a goofy face. "I'll be the court jester."

"Thanks," Elizabeth said, smiling happily. "I have to ask some of the other kids. Meet me over by the slide."

Elizabeth went all over the playground. Everyone in their class knew about Kelly's problem, and all the kids Elizabeth talked to said they would help.

"Hear ye, hear ye!" Elizabeth called out, clapping her hands for attention. "Make way for Her Majesty, Queen Kelly!"

Jessica's face lit up. She understood right away what Elizabeth was doing. "This way, Your Highness," she said. She bowed to Kelly and swept out her arm.

"What are you doing?" Kelly asked, laughing.

Elizabeth's and Jessica's friends marched over to Kelly. The boys bowed and the girls curtsied. Then they led the way to the slide. "Your throne, Madam," Elizabeth said.

Grinning from ear to ear, Kelly climbed the ladder and sat on the top of the slide. "What do I do now?" she asked.

"You just sit there and be Queen of the Park," Todd said. "Do you have any royal orders?"

61

"Free ice cream and candy bars for every-one," Kelly announced.

The kids all cheered. "Hey, I have a joke for you, Your Majesty," Winston said. "Why didn't the chicken cross the road?"

"Why?" Kelly asked.

"Because it was chicken." Winston slapped his knee and laughed loudly.

Elizabeth noticed a crumpled ball of tin foil on the ground. When she uncrumpled it, it was long enough to make a crown. She quickly twisted it into shape.

"Your royal crown," she said. She climbed up the ladder of the slide and put the ring of shiny foil on Kelly's head.

"Queen Kelly," Jessica said, getting down on one knee. "Will you please give a ball for all the princes and princesses?"

Kelly put one finger on her chin and

thought. "I think we should have a ball every day."

"Do you have any other announcements?" Eva asked.

Kelly nodded. "I am making school against the law."

Everyone cheered again.

"And eggplant, Brussels sprouts, and all the other yucky vegetables are against the law, too," Kelly went on. "We'll only have peas and corn at the castle."

"Court Jester, tell another joke," Ken said.

While Winston clowned around for the group, Elizabeth looked across the park. She wanted to see if any of their other classmates were arriving.

A car stopped at the park gates, and Aunt Laura and Uncle Greg got out. Elizabeth felt her heart do a swan dive. They weren't supposed to arrive until the next morning, on Thanksgiving Day.

Were they coming early because they had bad news? Elizabeth wondered nervously. Kelly and the others were still laughing at Winston's jokes. That meant no one else had seen Kelly's parents yet.

Then Kelly let out a gasp. She was staring straight at her mother and father. "Oh, no," she whispered.

CHAPTER 10

Giving Thanks

All the kids stopped talking at once. Jessica looked over to see what was wrong. When she saw Aunt Laura and Uncle Greg, she grabbed Elizabeth's hand. "Uh-oh," she said softly. "Those are Kelly's parents," she told the others.

Looking very worried, Kelly slid down the slide and ran over to the gate. Everyone watched in silence while she kissed and hugged her parents. Jessica wished she could hear what they were saying.

"Liz! Jessica!" Aunt Laura called, waving them over.

Jessica grabbed her sister's hand, and they hurried toward the gate. "Hi," Jessica said timidly.

"Hello, girls. We just wanted to let you know that we're going to drive Kelly back to your house," Aunt Laura explained. "We'll see you there later."

"OK," Elizabeth said, looking wide-eyed at their cousin.

Kelly and her parents got into the car and drove away.

"They must have bad news," Jessica said, shaking her head. "Why else would they come early?"

"I don't know," Elizabeth said. "Maybe we should just go home right now."

They walked slowly back to the group. "We're going home," Jessica said in a gloomy tone.

"Bye," Eva said softly. "I hope you have a good Thanksgiving."

Jessica gulped. She had a feeling their Thanksgiving was going to be terrible.

Jessica and Elizabeth were silent as they walked home. They didn't want to talk about the bad news Aunt Laura and Uncle Greg were probably telling Kelly. When they arrived at their front door they stopped for a moment.

Elizabeth took a deep breath. "I guess we should go in," she said, opening the door.

Jessica didn't want to go, but she followed her sister into the living room. Jessica was afraid to look at anyone.

"Girls, you're back," Mrs. Wakefield said.

Jessica looked quickly at Kelly. Their cousin was sitting on the couch between Aunt Laura and Uncle Greg, and they were all smiling.

"We're not getting a divorce," Aunt Laura explained.

"You're not?" Jessica couldn't believe her ears.

Uncle Greg shook his head. "We still have some problems to figure out, but we're going to give it another try."

Jessica and Elizabeth ran to the couch and hugged Kelly. "I'm so glad," Jessica whispered.

"We really want to be a family," Aunt Laura said. She kissed Kelly. "We love Kelly so much, and we really think we can work things out so we can all stay together."

Kelly was sniffling and smiling at the same time. She couldn't talk at all.

"You're the most important person in our lives," Kelly's father reminded her, giving her another kiss on the head.

Mrs. Wakefield was glowing with happiness. "This is going to be a very special Thanksgiving."

Everyone was in a joyful mood on Thanksgiving Day. Elizabeth, Jessica, and Kelly set the table with the good china and silverware and fancy napkins. Steven helped make the mashed potatoes, Uncle Greg carved the turkey, Aunt Laura made the salad, Mr. Wakefield cooked the rice, and Mrs. Wakefield supervised everything.

"I'm so hungry I could eat the whole turkey," Steven said as they all sat down. He reached for the dish of cranberry sauce.

"Just a minute, Steven," Mr. Wakefield said, holding up one hand. "You know the rules."

"It's our tradition," Jessica explained to

Kelly. "We take turns saying what we're thankful for."

"I know what *I'm* thankful for," Kelly said. She smiled at her parents. "The best thing in the world. Having a family that loves me."

The Wakefields all cheered as Kelly's parents both leaned over and kissed her.

When they had each taken a turn giving thanks, it was time for the feast to begin. Jessica ate so much that she had to undo the button on her skirt.

"Does that mean you don't want a third helping, Jessica?" Mr. Wakefield asked.

"Not for me, Dad," Jessica answered. "I'm ready to explode."

"I want thirds and then fourths," Steven said, holding up his plate.

As Uncle Greg cut more slices of turkey, the telephone rang. Mr. Wakefield got up to

answer it. Jessica wondered who would call them on Thanksgiving Day.

"That was Mr. Wilkins," Mr. Wakefield said, returning to the table.

"Todd's father?" Elizabeth asked.

Jessica noticed that Kelly was grinning, and her eyes were twinkling. "It's the secret," Kelly said.

"Really? What is it?" Jessica asked excitedly.

Mr. Wakefield laughed. "The Wilkinses are inviting us to go with them on their ski vacation. The chalet they're renting is big enough for all of us."

"Skiing? Great!" Steven shouted. "I can't wait."

"We'll see snow for the very first time, Jessica said.

"And we'll all go speeding down the

slopes," Elizabeth said, getting more excited by the second.

"Whoa! We have to discuss it, first," Mrs. Wakefield reminded them. "You kids have never gone skiing before. There's a lot to learn."

Jessica smiled. "I told Todd he'd fall down and turn into a big snowball."

"Maybe we will, too," Elizabeth said. "Todd's a lot of fun. This trip is going to be great!"

Will Todd be as much fun as Elizabeth thinks? Find out in Sweet Valley Kids #25, LEFT-OUT ELIZABETH

SWEET VALLEY KIDS

Jessica and Elizabeth have had lots of adventures in *Sweet Valley High* and *Sweet Valley Twins*...now read about the twins at age seven! You'll love all the fun that comes with being seven—birthday parties, playing dress-up, class projects, putting on puppet shows and plays, losing a tooth, setting up lemonade stands, caring for animals and much more! It's all part of SWEET VALLEY KIDS. Read them all!

☐	SURPRISE! SURPRISE! #1	15758-2	$2.75/$3.25
☐	RUNAWAY HAMSTER #2	15759-0	$2.75/$3.25
☐	THE TWINS' MYSTERY TEACHER # 3	15760-4	$2.75/$3.25
☐	ELIZABETH'S VALENTINE # 4	15761-2	$2.75/$3.25
☐	JESSICA'S CAT TRICK # 5	15768-X	$2.75/$3.25
☐	LILA'S SECRET # 6	15773-6	$2.75/$3.25
☐	JESSICA'S BIG MISTAKE # 7	15799-X	$2.75/$3.25
☐	JESSICA'S ZOO ADVENTURE # 8	15802-3	$2.75/$3.25
☐	ELIZABETH'S SUPER-SELLING LEMONADE #9	15807-4	$2.75/$3.25
☐	THE TWINS AND THE WILD WEST #10	15811-2	$2.75/$3.25
☐	CRYBABY LOIS #11	15818-X	$2.75/$3.25
☐	SWEET VALLEY TRICK OR TREAT #12	15825-2	$2.75/$3.25
☐	STARRING WINSTON EGBERT #13	15836-8	$2.75/$3.25
☐	JESSICA THE BABY-SITTER #14	15838-4	$2.75/$3.25
☐	FEARLESS ELIZABETH #15	15844-9	$2.75/$3.25
☐	JESSICA THE TV STAR #16	15850-3	$2.75/$3.25
☐	CAROLINE'S MYSTERY DOLLS #17	15870-8	$2.75/$3.25
☐	BOSSY STEVEN #18	15881-3	$2.75/$3.25
☐	JESSICA AND THE JUMBO FISH #19	15936-4	$2.75/$3.25
☐	THE TWINS GO TO THE HOSPITAL #20	15912-7	$2.75/$3.25
☐	THE CASE OF THE SECRET SANTA (SVK Super Snooper #1)	15860-0	$2.95/$3.50